BURY MY HEART AT
Jones Beach

BURY MY HEART AT
Jones Beach

FRANCIS JOHN BALDUCCI

THE LIBRARY OF CONGRESS
Control Number: 1-1824499731

Balducci, Francis John, 1964–
bury my heart at jones beach / Francis John Balducci

ISBN 0692313141
ISBN-13 978-0-692-31314-5

Front and rear cover designs, images and elements by the author.

Printed in the United States of America.

Dedication

To Robert "Bobby" Kratenstein who
always does the right thing.

When the blood in your veins returns to the sea, and the earth in your bones returns to the ground, perhaps then you will remember that this land does not belong to you, it is you who belongs to this land.

Native American quote

Prologue

They are typical Long Island homes, encased in typical aluminum siding, carefully arranged in a typical Long Island neighborhood. White painted and antiseptic. Rectangles of well-manicured lawns are surrounded by the palest cement walks and the blackest of asphalt. Young sugar maple trees stand at attention on either side of the quiet street. And the neighbors?—typical suburban.

In the weekday mornings, men in pressed suits and thrown-back power ties sip coffee from travel mugs as they hastily maneuver down their driveways, around skateboards and hula hoops, to where shiny sedans await. The wives, while inside, tend to the waking children who make their best attempts to fake illness so that they may be allowed to stay home from school.

Life is there.

By contrast, there is one house on the block, empty and uninhabited. Months of nature's unchecked growth sprouts around it. It is listed as a bank foreclosure property, but it is under contract. In a real estate office not far away, a newly-married couple is enthusiastic to move into that house and start a family of their own. They are equally as eager to achieve well-manicured lawns.

Life will happen there.

* * *

Six miles to the south, the cold and brackish North Atlantic waves lap against the shore of Jones Beach.

The beach park is approaching its post-season. Patches of brown foam deposited by the waves boast meandering shapes; multitudes of broken shells are strewn everywhere. Gusts of wind whistle along the empty dunes as gulls hobble about and scavenge for the last morsels the beachgoers left behind. Near the boardwalk, park workers take a break from scouring the landscape for trash by smoking cigarettes and chatting next to a beach utility cart. In the not-so-far distance, red-brick bathhouses ascend as ancient temples to the gods of bathing. In the farther distance, a tall, brick tower looms in a fog watching over the beach park as a solemn sentinel.

On the boardwalk, some restaurants and shops are still open to cater to the dwindling patrons. Ice cream and hot dogs are on the menu while baseball caps and tee-shirts are still available. A sign over one shop reads, "Summer Clearance." Sunrise gives this venue a particularly somber look for the late-season stragglers and joggers.

Beyond the boardwalk, the harsh sound of a tow truck's chains on the side of the parkway cut through the salty, morning air. The truck driver sleepily tends to a weathered, solitary car while he sips his coffee from a paper cup. After the truck exits with its haul, the setting returns to quiet.

* * *

A derelict man rummages through a ship-funnel-shaped trash can on the boardwalk. Although he is in his mid-thirties in age, his appearance is poor; his hair is unmanaged and his curled beard traps small remnants of dead skin; his shirt is dingy with sweat marks, and his grease-spotted gray pants are held up by thick, brown twine; his shoes are worn at the tops with the soles nearly gone.

His nearby shopping cart contains additional clothes, empty soda bottles, and plastic bags—all that he owns. He is hungry, but he has become used to the feeling.

He finds a partially-eaten hot dog bun and crams it into his mouth without much thought. While chewing, he continues to rummage until he sees a small, shiny object near the bottom of the trash can. He quickly recovers it. He stops chewing as he inspects it. It is a compass ring. He carefully places it on his pinky finger and resumes chewing and foraging.

Later that same day, the derelict takes advantage of the open men's restroom. As he sits in one of the toilet stalls, he reads the words written with a marker: LIVE THE LIFE YOU'VE DREAMED. As he stands to leave the stall, he reads a solitary word written with a different, broader marker: RELAX. He stares at the word and thinks for a moment.

* * *

The derelict sits on a thick, faux-wooden bench on the boardwalk as he watches the ocean surf. While the wind blows his hair across his forehead, his mind underneath draws a deep blank; at times he struggles to capture a thought. He takes a breath and tastes the air as it fills his lungs. He closes his eyes as he exhales, and surrenders to his unconsciousness.

His mind is dominated by various images. Among them, he envisions a young man in a tuxedo raising a Champaign glass. He labors to recognize him and, although the man's smile looks familiar, he cannot fully identify him.

He then wakes with a jolt to find a young boy standing and facing him, just looking at him. The boy sustains an empathetic expression of sorts. The derelict looks back at the boy expecting him to change his expression in some way or say something. The derelict then hears a woman's voice emerge from over his shoulder.

"*Billy!* There you are!"

The mother comes into the derelict's view and quickly takes the boy by the hand and drags him away. While the derelict watches them hastily leave, he sees the woman look back at him in disgust. The derelict then closes his eyes again in hopes of unraveling the mystery of his mental images.

A beautiful, young woman rises from the surf. She has long, straight hair and soft features. Her long gown slowly flows into the waves below her. He is certain that he knows her; she is so familiar. He is captivated by her beauty until fire emerges around her head. She screams as a fiery whirlwind engulfs her and, before he can call out to her, she quickly dissolves into dust and is carried away by the wind.

He awakens with tears occupying his eyes. He then turns to his cart and digs for a half-eaten bag of chips that he found earlier that afternoon.

Chapter One

Meandering about the boardwalk, pushing his cart, the derelict stops at another garbage can. It is his twelfth such stop thus far today. He carefully rummages through it and finds the remains of a stale jumbo pretzel. He holds it carefully while he retrieves a mustard packet from one of his plastic bags. Upon finding one, he sits on a bench to eat. The people stare at the derelict as he prepares his meal, but they quickly turn away when he looks up. The derelict pauses for just a moment to study them with the hope of finding a friendly expression. He doesn't receive one.

With something in his belly, he decides to venture west to the other side of the beach park. It is there where he finds a small Indian village that perhaps serves as a cultural attraction for the park goers.

The Indian village attraction occupies a rectangular parcel of land approximately three-hundred twenty-four feet by one-hundred forty-nine feet. On this land sit tipis, some arraigned in a circle in the center while smaller ones are aligned in rows of three on either side. All are well constructed of animal hide and thick, roughly-cut wooden poles and strong rope.

It appears as though the few villagers left behind from the summer season are in preparation for the cold winter months. An old man who appears to be a tribal elder—a man with a bold look—sees the derelict. When the derelict sees the elder, he is amazed at his appearance. The elder raises his hand high in greeting. The derelict returns the gesture and walks away in the opposite direction.

* * *

Amir is a boardwalk shopkeeper. His shop is located on the west end of the beach park. He sells a sundry of park promotional souvenir items such as baseball caps, tee-shirts, and refrigerator magnets. He occasionally sees the derelict and, each time that he does, he offers him an inhospitable expression. Since their eyes met for the first time and all other times thereafter, the derelict has managed to not make eye contact with Amir out of respect.

* * *

The setting sun glimmers off the orange and brown awnings of Amir's shop. The derelict sits on a nearby bench. The shop is open despite the absence of people. From the direction of a small parking lot, however, a man wearing a wool cap quickly emerges on to the boardwalk and hastily looks around. He sees the derelict but is not concerned about his presence. He adjusts an odd bulge in his jacket pocket and enters Amir's shop. The derelict sees this and quickly becomes concerned. The derelict stealthily moves to the shop window and looks inside. He sees the man walk down one aisle and then down another. He sees Amir emerge from behind his counter and say something to the man.

"Sir, I'm closing in five minutes," Amir said.

The derelict suddenly sees the man draw a small pistol and, with this man's finger on the trigger, he shouts something. Amir raises his hands slowly and carefully.

"Money! All of it! *Quickly*, asshole!" the man said while the pistol shakes in his hand.

Over the robber's shoulder, the derelict enters the store undetected. He quietly lifts a heavy, oversized mug from a shelf behind him and strikes the robber with great force to the back of his head. The pistol fires into the ceiling as the robber drops to the floor. The robber's eyes roll to the back of his head while the derelict pries the pistol from his hand and safely tosses it at Amir's feet. Amir's and the derelict's eyes meet for a moment. Just before Amir could say something, the derelict puts the mug back on the shelf and quickly leaves the shop.

The police arrive in nearly ten minutes. They find the robber on the floor tied behind his back by a red-white-and-blue-colored bikini bottom, groaning in pain. One officer places handcuffs on the robber while the other officer talks with Amir.

"So, let me get this right," the officer said. "You threw a mug at his head and knocked him out?"

"Um, yes, officer."

"Do you realize how stupid that sounds?"

"Yes, sir; I am stupid. I am very stupid."

"You're no hero! You could've gotten killed. And, for what? You're married?"

"Yes, officer. I have two baby daughters."

The officer shakes his head. "Don't be a friggin' hero again! Next time, you give the robber what he wants and then call us. Let us do our job."

"Yes, officer. I will."

"Close your shop and meet us at the seventh precinct. You have some papers to sign."

As Amir leaves his shop, he looks around for the derelict. He is nowhere to be seen.

Chapter Two

A chill dominates the October air. The derelict sits nearly rolled into a ball on a boardwalk bench while tightly clutching the collar of his coat. His drab-colored Panama Jack cap, which he found blowing on the sand, is affixed firmly to his head.

Asleep, he dreams of a toddler girl riding a pink, flowery miniature car on the boardwalk. The image is intermingled with that of a young woman—the same woman he envisioned weeks before. She smiles broadly and claps her hands at the girl, but no sound is heard. Her face quickly displays a horrific look. The derelict sees the child propelled from her seat; the woman screams; both are engulfed in flames.

The derelict abruptly awakens. He has tears in his eyes. He wipes his running nose and closes his eyes again. He thinks his vision is a sign that death is upon him, and he welcomes its arrival.

* * *

"Hey! *Hey!*"

Amir shakes the derelict in an attempt to wake him.

"Sir, *please* wake up!"

The derelict slowly opens his eyes. When his eyes focus on Amir's face he sits back startled.

"No, please! I want to help you—let me help you!" Amir said.

The muscles in the derelict's frozen face relax a little. Amir wipes the ice crystals from the derelict's brow as he assists the man to his feet. Amir gestures to the direction of his shop.

"I want you to come with me. I want to take you to where it is warm. Please, come."

The derelict struggles to convey words.

"My cart."

"Leave it; you no longer have any need for it."

* * *

Amir turns the key to his shop while he holds the derelict by his elbow.

"Come inside," he said. "I have food."

They both enter the shop. Amir closes the door and locks it. He turns to the derelict.

"My name is Amir. Are you hungry?"

The derelict nods slowly.

"Okay," he said with a smile; "I have my wife's cooking." He takes out a food container and opens it carefully to show him.

"I hope you like Persian."

The derelict looks at it and smiles.

"It is bean stew," Amir said.

"Ghormeh sabzi," the derelict responded.

"Yes, ghormeh sabzi," Amir said with surprise. "You know of this?"

The derelict pauses and takes a moment to reflect; he almost looks puzzled. Amir tries to redirect the derelict's attention.

"Let me warm this up for you."

Amir places the container into a small microwave oven and activates it.

"Here, I want to show you something." Amir leads the derelict to the back of the shop. They walk through a doorway of dangling beads.

"This place is for you," Amir said. He gestures to a small bed. "This is where you may sleep. The sheets are clean, and I have some clothes for you."

The derelict sees various tee-shirts and sweat pants on a wooden dresser.

"If the clothes don't fit, I have more." Amir giggles. "I have much more."

The derelict picks up one of the tee-shirts and holds it to his chest. On its front, it prominently displays the words, JONES BEACH.

The microwave beeps.

"Oh, good!" Amir smiles. "It is time for dinner. Let me bring it in. In the meantime, change your clothes. There is a bathroom in the next room with all that you need."

"Thank you," the derelict said in an almost inaudible voice.

"Thank *you*," Amir responded. "And you are welcome." Amir pauses and looks in his eyes. "What is your name?"

The derelict searches in his mind.

"It is all right. You will tell me once you find yourself. Until then, you will remain my friend, yes? Here is the key. You may come and go as you like. I will get your dinner."

Amir leaves the room. The derelict takes off his coat and sits on the bed. He looks up at a poster taped to the wall. It's composed of the image of an attractive Middle-Eastern model wearing a swimsuit.

* * *

The next morning, the derelict is greeted by Amir and a steaming cup of strong coffee sitting in the center of a bright, silver tray.

"Good morning, my friend," Amir said with a smile. "I have people that I would like you to meet."

The derelict sits up and makes an attempt to fix his grossly-unmanaged hair. He wipes his eyes to remove some crud, and he labors to clear his throat with a few coughs. He picks up the cup of coffee and takes a sip of it.

Waiting in the shop is a graceful-looking woman and two young girls. Amir and the derelict emerge from the back room. Amir makes the introduction.

"Sir, I would like you to meet my wife, Kiana. And, these are our daughters, Irisa and Babuk."

The woman steps up to the derelict and speaks in a clear voice.

"Thank you for saving my husband," she said while trying to contain her emotions.

The older daughter, at nine years old, steps up to the derelict. She gestures for him to kneel down, and he complies.

"Thank you for saving my father's life," she said. She then kisses him on the cheek. "I'll call you 'Tahmin.' It means 'brave'."

He smiles at the girl. She smiles back.

FRANCIS JOHN BALDUCCI

Chapter Three

Snow covers the boardwalk and sand dunes as far as the eye can see; the precipitation is thick and heavy, especially offshore. It is the peak of winter.

The snow-topped tipis offer a striking appearance. Fires are set in various places to warm the tribal members who remain. Most members, however, have moved to nearby homes while others spend the winter months in Florida. One member, a man of some affluence, owns the sole village horse, Wanagi. Every winter, he takes this bold, white steed to his Virginia ranch. All return just before the start of the summer season.

On the boardwalk, the tribal elder in a traditional winter robe stands overlooking the village. After completing a Merokee prayer that he softly whispered to the icy wind, he notices a familiar man looking at him—the derelict—but this time the man is sporting a cleaner appearance. The elder turns to him.

"Kwe-kwe," the derelict said while raising his hand. The elder is surprised at this and offers a broad smile.

"Kwe-kwe," the elder returned with his hand raised. "You know Algonquin."

The derelict thinks for a moment, but all he can do is smile back.

"My name is Big Feather."

"My name is Tahmin," the derelict said with lips numb with cold.

"Hello, Tom. I am a Merokee chief." Big Feather gestures over the land with one hand. "I serve as the village leader."

"It is a fine village, chief."

"It is all that we have now."

"All that you have?"

"Tom, the people here are not only Algonquin or Shinnecock; we are from all nations. We live in harmony like grains of sands and, like the sea, we accept all people."

"You have lived here all your life?"

"I grew up further east. As a boy, I learned much of life through the nature around me: the stars taught me about the smallness of my spirit while animal bites strengthened my body. My tribe taught me about love, until, one day, I saw her."

"Who?" Tahmin asked with interest.

"The woman who would teach me about a special kind of love. I married Little Mouth here. It has been three decades now, and I remember it all as though it was only three moons ago. I remember every bead on her wedding dress. I remember every word her father, Black Horn, told me on the night of our wedding."

"What did he tell you?"

"He told me to never hold on too tightly to what you love—to hold it like a new sparrow. He told me that if I let life's path lead me, I would be chief like him. And, here I am."

"Do you believe that your people will endure?"

"Young Tom, for generations Indians have lived throughout this great island, thick like fleas on a bear's ass. We are confined only here, and we will defend our right to survive by force if that is needed."

"Confined?"

"By the soldiers, of course."

Tahmin pauses. "Of course."

"You seem lost, my friend. I can see it in your eyes."

Tahmin pauses again. "Madjacin, chief," he said.

"Madjacin, Tom. Maybe one day you will make your journey home."

"Big Feather!" a small Indian woman standing in front of a grand tipi said in a loud voice.

"Coming, wife."

Big Feather quickly slips away.

* * *

In the room in the rear of Amir's shop, Tahmin dreams on his small bed.

In one dream, he sees Big Feather wearing what appears to be his summer robe. The chief is sitting still on the ground in front of his tipi. A spear adorned with black feathers leans against the tipi entrance, and Wanagi is grazing nearby covered almost completely in war paint. The image is ghostly and sublime.

"My people," he heard the chief say. "Will you

join the fight?"

"I don't know, sir—I just don't know," Tahmin answered.

"Your fight is *our* fight, my friend."

"But, what do we fight for?"

The chief pauses. As his features fade into the wind, he answers.

"Identity..."

His final dream is more detailed. In it, he sees the face of the elusive young woman that he has envisioned for the last few months. He concentrates. Her facial features become increasingly clear; he sees her eyes, her complexion. He somehow knows her. He tries to speak and, as he does manage to say something, she looks away. She gracefully turns, and is gone as quickly as she appeared. As his anxiety rises, he quickly thinks of one word: RELAX.

Tahmin slowly opens his eyes. His first sight is the face of the Middle-Eastern model in the poster. He then looks around the room, at the small lamp, and at the dresser. After a moment, he lifts the covers and rises.

While brushing his teeth, he hears Amir enter the shop.

"I have donuts!" he heard Amir say.

Tahmin stops brushing and looks deeply at his image in the fogging mirror. His mind wanders back to the woman. He thinks about her so intensely that he fails to realize the overflowing sink until the hot water pours onto his bare feet.

"Ouch!" he exclaimed.

"Are you okay in there?"

"I'm fine. I'm just finishing up."

"All right. The donuts are fresh."

"Thank you. I'm on my way."

Tahmin resumes his gaze into the mirror. He takes water into his mouth with his hand and rinses.

He then turns off the light.

Chapter Four

"This design did not sell at all," Amir said while holding up a tee-shirt as he takes post-season inventory. "No one likes starfish."

Tahmin listens while chewing a bite of a jelly donut. Sugar glistens on his lips; jelly accumulates at the corners of his mouth. He can't think of a response, so he keeps eating.

"Sharks!" Amir continues. "People like sharks—they always have—better than dolphins. See?" Amir holds up another tee-shirt.

Tahmin thinks. He then swallows.

"Mermaids? No. Sailboats? No. Not even stingrays. Sometimes I never know what sells until the season has already started. And, by that time, it is too late."

"What about tipis?" he offered.

Amir pauses. "On a beach?"

"Yes. Maybe."

Amir stops working. "You saw the village."

"I met with Big Feather. He is concerned about his people."

"And, you take him seriously?"

"He spoke of soldiers."

"He spoke of what?"

"Soldiers."

"Tahmin, Big Feather's concerns are in his head. The land has served as an attraction to beachgoers since the 1950s."

"It has? That's a long time."

"No developer will touch it because most of the island's recreational land is owned by the Shinnecock Nation. So, they are well protected." He resumes work. "Seahorses! None sold!"

"Maybe I can help him. He seems quite sane."

"Big Feather sees himself as a warrior who seeks his next battle—on the island, on the beach—in his head. Don't trouble yourself with this, my friend."

"I don't know."

"Please, have another donut." Amir throws a tee-shirt over his shoulder.

* * *

Spring quickly approaches; the snow is all gone, and much of the sand has eroded.

As Tahmin steps out of the shop and deeply takes in the morning air, he notices some workers arriving to prepare the beach park for the upcoming season. His first thought is to visit the village to witness the return of the tribal members that were away for the winter.

The once-covered tipis now boast painted images of bison and elk. While Tahmin watches from the boardwalk, he marvels at such art. He turns to see the coming members, all dressed in colorful Indian clothing.

They trickle into the village, almost orderly, and approach Big Feather standing in front of his tipi. As a sign of respect, they present a gesture of salutation and a gift to him as he welcomes them home. Big Feather appears to bless each of them as they approach.

As the numbers grow, Tahmin becomes increasingly impressed. He observes embraces, the exchanges of gifts, and blessings. He sees a gathering coalesce into one family. He cannot turn his eyes away.

Shortly after their arrival, some villagers proceed to gather planks that were left over from the boardwalk's renovation for firewood. Others grab spears and walk to the surf to fish. Others haul baskets of corn and gourds.

When Tahmin turns back toward Big Feather, he sees a young man approach him and Little Mouth. Both elders embrace and kiss him. The chief takes the youth's face in his hands and smiles at him. They exchange words, but Tahmin is too far away to hear what they are saying. They embrace again. The young man then introduces them to a girl companion. She is dressed in ceremonial colors and beads. They smile at her.

Also accompanying the young man are three male Indians. One is a short, warrior type. The other is tall and strong, but with a gentle face. The last one looks sleepy and clumsy. All are beautifully adorned and respectful toward Big Feather.

By noon, the congregation culminates into a grand welcoming ceremony. Scattered open fires are lit roasting elk and deer carcasses. Other fires roast fish and corn. The billowing smoke rises high above the village and carries with it tantalizing aromas.

In a huge circle that encompasses the entire village, the villagers chant to the beat of drums and rattles. All are dressed in various traditional Indian clothing that include bonnets, head bands, skins, feathers, fringed leggings, and moccasins. Some accent themselves with shells, shark teeth, wampum, mother-of-pearl, and arrowheads, while others decorate themselves with deer antlers, turtle shells, pelts, and raccoon skulls. Many of the women hold hawk- and peacock-feathered fans while men carry fishing spears and tomahawks. All participants are brightly colored and impressive.

Tahmin, while remaining clandestine, becomes deeply intrigued and enchanted with what he sees. He views people of all ages in solemn celebration. He witnesses harmony and community.

Before the villagers feast on their bounty, Big Feather mounts Wanagi. Little Mouth hands him a ceremonial tomahawk. He then addresses the gathering.

"My people. Welcome home!"

Cheers erupt.

"Today is a good day." Big Feather gestures to the young man. "My son, Four Winds, has returned and he has found love with Red Leaf, daughter of Gray Smoke and Slow River."

More cheers burst as the couple wave and as Big Feather clears his throat.

"We gather here today after our long winter slumber, with the blessings of the great creator and the spirits of the earth, to reaffirm ourselves in this sacred place as our ancestors have done before us. The sands and every glistening shell are our mother, and spread across these dunes are the bones of our fathers. The ocean is our sister, and the salt it contains is the same salt that courses through our veins. The wind is our brother that carries the voice of our people. And, that voice says that we are all one family."

The villagers cheer loudly.

"My people," Big Feather continues. "The great spirit has spoken to my heart without words. He says that we will be victorious in opposing the bluecoats!"

Despite the fact that the villagers are puzzled by the comment, they continue to cheer. Little Mouth, as though it was planned, conveys a statement in a very loud voice.

"Let the feast begin!"

The villagers cheer again.

Tahmin, thinking that the time was right, heads back to the shop where Amir—along with Amir's wife's cooking—awaits him.

* * *

"It was amazing!" Tahmin told Amir while eating a bowl of soup. "The music, the dancing, and the bright colors."

"Hmm, I see," Amir responded. "I've seen it last year. It is a sight."

"Yeah, but Amir, it was so much more than that. It was family."

"It is a beach attraction and nothing more."

"I think you are wrong."

"Well, I think that you may be taking this too seriously, Tahmin."

"I don't know."

"Finish your soup before it gets cold. Abgoosht bozbash tastes terrible when it is cold."

* * *

April ushers in mild weather. But, it also brings about concerns for the villagers.

A secret plan is being considered by Benjamin Archer, the elected leader of the Shinnecock Nation's Council of Elders, to demolish the Indian village to make room for a more profitable form of recreation and entertainment. Archer is very wealthy and powerful, and he has quickly become a close friend of casino developer and financier, Ronald Drake, who is the principle owner of Drake Casino Resorts.

To garner publicity and public support to prevent the village from being demolished, the villagers conduct a rally on the boardwalk. Leading the rally is Big Feather and Little Mouth. By their side is their son, Four Winds, and his girlfriend, Red Leaf.

The other tribal members in attendance include Four Winds' three associates: the short brave named Leaping Frog, the towering, gentle-faced warrior named Juicy Fruit, and one Indian who is not regarded as very bright named Sleeping Elk.

Big Feather asserts himself before the crowd.

"We will protect our land to our last warrior," he exclaimed. "Let no brave return alive!" But, not all villagers take him completely serious.

Unknown to Big Feather, hidden in the audience is Archer. He appears slightly nervous while listening to Big Feather's words as he attempts to conceal his face to prevent him from being recognized.

Chapter Five

Tahmin sits on a bench on the boardwalk, sleeping. He falls in and out of a dream. The dream then takes hold of his unconsciousness and transforms itself into another attack—this time more violent and more detailed.

During the episode, he sees the image of a young man in a tuxedo. The man smiles at him as he sees him raise a Champagne glass in a toast. Tahmin believes that he knows this man, but he can't fully remember him. He calls out to the man, but he doesn't respond. After a moment, the smile leaves the man's face. The man is suddenly stricken with grief. The glass he is holding drops to the floor and shatters into glistening, tiny fragments. Tahmin then feels his own body pulled down as though he is being dragged under. He reaches up, but he doesn't even see his outstretched arm. Nothingness surrounds him.

The nightmare shifts. He sees the familiar young woman. This time, she is crying—screaming. Fire and black smoke surrounds her as she gasps for air. He then hears the cries of a child; he turns to locate her, but the child is nowhere to be seen. He turns again toward the woman, but she is gone. He tries to calm his mind: he whispers to himself, "Relax." He awakens to find himself in tears.

* * *

Police officers and parks officials converge on the Indian village, one with papers in his hand. They approach Big Feather standing in front of his tipi.

"Sir," the lead official said; "I have an order for you and these people to vacate these premises by twelve noon tomorrow." He hands Big Feather the papers.

"I am Chief Big Feather, and these are my people," he said in a dignified tone. One parks official in the rear grasps his mouth in an attempt to hold back laughter. Big Feather sees this. He looks away and sees a tomahawk leaning against a log.

"Uh, chief," the official continues; "This is a bona fide court order administered by a judge. Now, you may appeal this, but for now the order stands. You must leave. Otherwise, you will be removed by force. We don't want any trouble. Good day, sir."

As the officials turn and walk away, Big Feather looks down at the papers. He reads them in horror. Many thoughts enter his mind, but leaving the village is not one of them. He slowly drops the pages into the fire.

* * *

The next day, a slew of blue-uniformed officers appear standing in a single rank at the borders of the village. They do not anticipate a fight, but they are prepared for any resistance nonetheless.

Tahmin, who was already awaken by the commotion, stands on the boardwalk watching intently and with grave concern.

The villagers stand by their tipis, some looking at Big Feather while others form in small groups. Only one grabs a weapon.

"I am ready to die!" Leaping Frog said.

"Put down that spear, now!" ordered Four Winds.

"Maybe we can take them," Sleeping Elk said while rubbing his eyes. "I'll get the horse."

"I said, put down that spear."

Leaping Frog drops the weapon and folds his arms.

"No horse?" Sleeping Elk said.

In a show of force, a police helicopter flies overhead.

"I don't think a horse will matter," Juicy Fruit said.

Red Leaf runs into Four Winds' arms. "I'm scared," she said.

Big Feather, with Little Mouth standing next to him holding his arm tightly, sees Four Winds. He then looks around with worry at the child villagers. Some villagers emerge from their tipis with spears and war clubs.

"Lay down your weapons!" Big Feather ordered. "We are outnumbered by the bluecoats and we must surrender."

A police officer approaches Big Feather cautiously. He stops in front of him.

"Sir, by order of the court, you are directed to vacate these premises. Do you understand?"

Big Feather reaches down and picks up a tomahawk.

The officer's eyes open wide with concern. He places his hand over his holstered pistol.

"This is Black Horn's tomahawk," Big Feather said. "It is the tomahawk of a chief. I give it to you now as a gesture of surrender."

"That won't be necessary," the officer, relieved, said. "You may take all of your belongings, but you must leave now."

* * *

Much of the village belongings have moved off the land. Some items that could not be removed— such as a few tipis—remain standing. The roar of an engine can be heard over a small hill. Emerging is a large, soot-breathing bulldozer. It rolls with great might onto the property demolishing everything in its path. The wide blade topples over the tipis as the thick tracks tear the skins to shreds.

The villagers helplessly watch the surreal scene. A tear runs down Big Feather's cheek. Tahmin, while witnessing the destruction from the boardwalk, is overcome with disgust and shame.

* * *

In less than two weeks, an outrageously colorful miniature golf course occupies the land. The course features themed scenes of a windmill with a large Dutchman figure, along with large sculptured figures of Christopher Columbus, George Washington, and an Indian chief with a raised hand.

The Indians have relocated on the beach not far from the course. They are camped out with the few tipis that they were able to take with them. They walk about despondently.

Little Mouth has not uttered a word since they relocated. Four Winds traveled to the city to consult with an attorney.

Big Feather can be seen perched on the highest hill praying. He looks up at the pale moon and regards the sight of it as a good omen.

Tahmin tries to muster up the courage to see Big Feather. But, he is so ashamed at what the white man did that he can't bear to pay the chief a visit.

Chapter Six

The summer season opens. The miniature golf course gleams in the sun with anticipation of large summer crowds.

From the boardwalk, Tahmin sees the Indian settlement beyond the picket fences. He knows he must find the courage to speak with Big Feather on the high hill. He decides that today is the day.

On the hill, Tahmin finds Big Feather sitting upright with his legs crossed. He wears black mourning beads prominently over his chest. His eyes are tightly shut.

"Big Feather?"

The chief appears to be in a deep trace and doesn't respond.

"Big Feather?" he said louder.

He opens his eyes and looks at him. "Greetings, Tom. Your presence lifts my heart."

"Big Feather, I am so sorry for what my people did to you and your people."

"The fault is not with you; I failed my people. The bluecoats possess great power. There was iron in their words. They led us on a road that goes nowhere."

"Is there anything that can be done?"

"My son went to the great city. He knows good people there who may help. I hope that help will come soon. We can only stay here for a short time. Then, we will be finished."

"What will become of you and Little Mouth?"

"We may move west," he said sadly.

"West?"

"Staten Island. But, until then, I will continue praying to my father and grandfathers."

Big Feather closes his eyes and resumes his prayers. As Tahmin turns and begins his walk down the hill, Big Feather says one more thing.

"It was good of you to visit, Tom. I hope to see you again, in this life or the next."

* * *

At Amir's shop, droves of visitors move about the aisles selecting hordes of items from hooks and shelves and bringing them to a noisy cash register. Amir smiles broadly while ringing up goods and answering simple questions. The shop experiences a surge in business as compared to previous seasons. Tahmin enters the shop.

"Yes, ma'am, nine dollars," Amir said. "Here is your change. Thank you, and come again." He sees Tahmin. "Come help! Please go in the back and get boxes of tee-shirts and ball caps. Hurry!"

Tahmin runs to the back and emerges with the boxes. Amir runs from behind the register to open the boxes and hang the articles.

"I have never needed an assistant," Amir said with a broad smile. "Wow!"

"What's going on?"

"Did you see the golf course? It is crammed full of people, and many of them are coming in here! They are buying everything!"

"Great, Amir," Tahmin said with concealed apprehension.

"I will need to increase my orders right away to restock. It is going to be my best season ever!" Amir steps back behind the register. "Okay, who is next? One at a time, please."

A thought enters Tahmin's mind; he speculates that the Indians may have lost all support from Amir and all the other shop keepers. He fears that all is lost for Big Feather and his tribe.

* * *

That night, Amir enthusiastically tallies his receipts. Tahmin sits near him sipping on a cup of black coffee.

"Seven... five, six, seven, eight, nine... eight... five, six... Oh!" Amir scribbles on some paper and holds it up. "Eight thousand, six-hundred, eleven dollars, and twenty-six cents." Amir smiles broadly.

"That's a lot?" Tahmin asked.

"That's a lot? That's the most that I have ever earned in a single day! And, this is the first day of the season!"

Tahmin takes a deep breath and puts down the coffee cup.

"But, what about the Indians?" he asked.

"What about them?"

"They lost their homes, their lands. What about them?"

"Tahmin, they were merely an attraction for visitors, nothing more. They were not bringing in more visitors, so they needed to go."

"Nothing more? These are people!" Tahmin said with excitement.

"You are my friend, but what you are saying is ridiculous!"

"White men—bluecoats—drove them out!"

"It was not a *real* village! What is wrong with you?"

"Nothing is wrong with me. In fact, I know who I am now: I am a human being!"

Amir takes a moment.

"You must go now," he said. "You must leave this place. If you have learned who you are, then I have fulfilled my obligation to you for saving my life."

"Okay, I will go now."

"Take with you whatever you need. Clothes? Whatever you want. Money?"

"I am grateful for all that you have done for me, Amir. But, now, I need nothing from you."

Tahmin places the key to the shop on the counter and leaves. The door behind him closes gently. Amir never looks up.

* * *

With nowhere else to go besides the boardwalk, Tahmin heads toward the settlement. He sees Four Winds sitting alone on the sand. He approaches him.

"I am a friend of your father's. How is Big Feather?"

Four Winds slowly looks up.

"My father prays. That is all he does."

"To his father and grandfathers?"

"No, to the great warrior god."

Tahmin displays a confused look.

"I went into the city to meet with a constitutional lawyer," Four Winds said while straightening up. "He said that there is nothing he can do. We may appeal this to the Council of Elders but, because of the high profits made over the weekend, we may never regain our land."

Drum beats are heard from the settlement.

"What is that?" Tahmin asked.

"It is the sound of our sacred war dance. We have decided to take back our land by force."

Chapter Seven

"A hole in one!" a man called out while puttering on the miniature golf course. His friends pat him on the back.

Another man places a ball down. Just before he putters, the ball slowly rolls away. He bends down, picks it up, and places it back into position. The ball rolls away again.

"Did you feel something?" a heavyset woman said.

All the puttering stops as the ground rumbles below their feet. The rumble increases steadily and quickly.

"Earthquake!" someone yelled.

Something rolls over the hill—something big. The golfers watch in amazement as an exhaust pipe stack slowly rises and belching black smoke. When they realize the bulldozer is headed directly for them, they become increasingly troubled. After the contraption clears the hill, they see a band of Indian brave stalking behind it. The golfers then run in horror.

In the cab operating the bulldozer is Four Winds. He is wearing full battle garb including a war bonnet with war paint on his face. Even the bulldozer is adorned with war paint in warhorse design. He cries out to the scurrying golfers while he raises a tomahawk.

Hurdling over the bulldozer is Leaping Frog. As soon as he lands on his feet, he sweeps his two fingers across his forehead and attacks the Dutchman figure. Juicy Fruit pushes over the windmill with great ease. Even with the highest of enthusiasm, Sleeping Elk experiences trouble taking down the George Washington figure. He resorts to breaking golf clubs over his knee.

Big Feather rides Wanagi above the action, directing the "battle" and providing inspiration—like a good chief. He sees that Tahmin has joined the fight.

"It is a good day to destroy a golf course!" Big Feather proclaimed loudly.

Tahmin did indeed join the invasion, but only to make certain that no one gets hurt. He is surprised at how much fun he is having. He doesn't remember the last time he ever laughed so hard. He turns around to see Four Winds using the bulldozer's ripper shank to tear the head of the Christopher Columbus' figure to pieces.

War chants are heard throughout the beach park. With every passing moment, the miniature golf course becomes increasingly demolished.

* * *

In the aftermath, much of what remains of the golf course is quickly pushed aside. It looks like a true warzone. Leaping Frog takes the wheel of the bulldozer to flatten the land while Juicy Fruit clears the area of large debris. The villagers rapidly work together to reconstruct the tipis, starting with the chief's.

Tahmin walks among the destruction being cleared away. He helps lift some pieces of fiberglass obstacles, broken golf clubs, and hundreds of golf balls. Big Feather sees him, walks over to him, and embraces him.

"Mino pijan!" Big Feather said.

"Meegwetch," Tahmin responded.

Big Feather smiles.

* * *

That night, Big Feather sits with Tahmin around a good fire. After the chief looks quietly at the flames for a few moments, he speaks.

"The great warrior god blessed us today. And you, my friend, fought like a true brave."

"I cleaned up a little," Tahmin said while looking down at the charring wood.

"Tom, you are brave, and you know much about the language and culture of my people. You are trusted above all white men, and you are as good as any red man that I have ever known. You have been lost within yourself for some time. But, now I believe you have been found. So, I have decided to take you as my son."

"I don't know what to say."

"Your new name is Pale Moon."

"I—I don't know what to say," he said while rubbing his abdomen.

"Are you hungry, my son? Little Mouth makes a raccoon stew that most people like."

"Yes, sir. I am."

"Then, let me feed your stomach now. Later, I will feed your mind."

Chapter Eight

In September, the air of Jones Beach is cooler, and the days are shorter.

The visiting public has decreased significantly and, since the Indians took back their village, the authorities have stayed away for reasons not known to anyone.

The derelict has been a resident of the beach park for a year, and now Pale Moon has his own tipi. Painted over its entrance is a moon.

His appearance has changed somewhat: his hair and beard are significantly trimmed and his overall look is cleaner and healthier.

While sitting on a log, feeding a fire, Pale Moon receives a visit from Four Winds.

"Kwe-kwe, nisaye," Four Winds said.

"Hello, brother," Pale Moon responded.

Four Winds sits next to him on the sand. He throws a small piece of wood on the fire.

"It has been a long summer it seems," he said.

Pale Moon just nods.

"I am happy we are brothers," Four Winds said. "I will leave soon, and it comforts me that you will remain to protect our father and mother. I know that you love them and they love you."

Pale Moon sits back and takes a deep breath. Four Winds looks at him carefully and senses something wrong.

"You seem troubled, brother. What inhabits your head?"

"Four Winds, I know no other family. Maybe I once did; but, I don't know. I know of love, and yet I have none. My arms yearn to hold someone, and yet I see no way to quench this desire."

"Like spots on a turtle, people surround you; yet, you are lonely."

"Yes."

Four Winds thinks for a moment. "I remember the first time I set my eyes on Red Leaf. I knew that she was the one that my heart has always dreamed of. I knew I had to have her. Her father, Gray Wolf, a holy man from the west, hated me. Until one day, I stood up to him. 'I will have your daughter,' I told him. He then hit me in my face so hard that I fell to the ground. When he offered to help me to my feet, I pushed his hand away. He respected me for that. And now, Red Leaf and I are together."

Pale Moon looks closely at him.

"My brother, you see?" Four Winds continues. "You must fight, fall, and rise for what you love. Who do you fight, fall, and rise for? When you answer this, then you will know."

Four Winds stands. "Madjacin, nisaye," he said.

"Madjacin, nisaye," Pale Moon responded as he watches him walk away.

* * *

That night, Pale Moon dreams inside his tipi. In one dream, he sees a gallery of different faces. He sees the familiar face of the man who had previously worn a tuxedo but, this time, he is much younger. The image fades away. He sees another face—that of the toddler girl. The image twists and contorts until it no longer resembles a face. Then, it is gone.

The familiar young woman then appears. His dream becomes lucid, and he struggles to wake from it. She grasps him to keep him in the dream. He feels the beads of sweat form on his conscious forehead, and he feels his hands close into tight fists. Yet, he cannot awaken. Outside his tipi while he continues to dream, he hears a loud shrill of a voice. It is Little Mouth calling out to Big Feather. Her call wakes him from his gripping dream.

When he emerges from the tipi, Little Mouth scolds him like any other mother would.

"Pale Moon, are you going to sleep all day?" she asked.

"What time is it?"

She looked up at the sun. "It is very late, after two." She looks at him carefully. Are you hungry?"

"No."

"Well, you will eat later. We will all eat later. The closing ceremony is tonight. So, fish with Sleeping Elk, and then gather firewood with Juicy Fruit."

Pale Moon nods as he scratches his head.

* * *

"If you catch more than me, white man, I will never fish again," he said while retrieving his spear from the water. He nearly slips on a huge boulder.

"Why do they call you Sleeping Elk?" Pale Moon asked.

"Because I am so good looking," he said without hesitation, and while wearing a cocky smile.

"No, really."

Sleeping Elk's smile fades from his lips.

"Oh, I'm sorry. It is a beautiful animal."

"Yes, it is," he asserts. "More than a bear."

"Most certainly."

They continue to fish.

"What about the fishing piers on the other side of the island?" Pale Moon asked.

"They don't allow spears. A big man there, he must have been the pier chief, chased me and Leaping Frog away." He points down with excitement. "Look, there!"

Pale Moon throws his spear, but it misses.

"Why don't we use fishing poles?" Pale Moon asked.

"Because that is the white man way, white man."

They continue to fish.

"Where will you go for the winter?" Pale Moon asked.

"Back to Manhattan. I am an accountant there."

"No, really?"

Sleeping Elk doesn't answer.

"I would never have guessed." Pale Moon thinks for a moment. "You know, I can see you as an accountant."

Before Sleeping Elk can respond, he sees another fish.

"That one is mine!" he insisted.

He throws the spear with such force that it imbeds itself deep in the sand, missing the fish.

"I got it!" Pale Moon declared.

He hurls his spear and impales the creature. He lifts the spear revealing his catch. He turns to Sleeping Elk to see the frustration in his face.

"Here," he said. He hands the spear to him. "This is your catch."

"No, you keep it. I'll go to my tipi to get my fishing pole."

Sleeping Elk walks off toward the village leaving Pale Moon with his mouth agape.

* * *

Later that afternoon, Pale Moon gathers firewood with Juicy Fruit.

"Where will you go for the winter?" Pale Moon asked the massive man.

"Nowhere. I am here all year round. What about you?"

"I don't know. I guess I'm staying." Pale Moon sees the large amount of firewood that Juicy Fruit can carry. "You are so tall. Have you ever played basketball?" he asked.

"No. I was never outgoing. I never spoke to anyone, ever, until I came here."

"You're outgoing now."

"A little. That's because of my father, Chief Big Feather. He took me in, and he insisted that my voice was always trapped deep inside my chest. One day, he punched me there. I let out a loud sound. I have been talking ever since."

"What were your first words?"

"I complained that our society suppresses individuality—something like that," Juicy Fruit said while still gathering.

Pale Moon stops gathering. "You're kidding."

"Well, it is true."

"I believe you, but, I just thought you'd say, 'Ouch!', or anything like that."

"Well, I did. Then I said our society suppresses individuality."

Pale Moon resumes gathering.

"Would you mind if I ask you one more question?"

"Sure, now that I can talk." Juicy Fruit smiles.

"How did you get your name?"

"I chew gum a lot, Wrigley's mainly. I like gum. Do you want gum?"

"I haven't had gum in as far back as I can remember."

The giant goes into his pocket and retrieves a pack of chewing gum. He gives Pale Moon a piece.

"Thank you," Pale Moon said. He carefully unwraps the gum and puts the piece into his mouth. He savors it as he chews.

"Good?" the Indian asked.

"Ah, Juicy Fruit."

* * *

The ceremonial final bonfire is in full swing. All are in attendance.

The smell of roasted meats and vegetables and the sound of tribal music fill the air. The villagers dance in celebration with traditional beauty. Leaping

Frog, however, doesn't seem to dance well. Sleeping Elk nearly burns himself while juggling torches, and Juicy Fruit shows off his strength by lifting huge logs over his head to the amazement of the children.

Around the huge fire, Pale Moon sits with Big Feather and Little Mouth. Pale Moon is still, almost entirely preoccupied and in deep thought, while Big Feather discreetly studies him.

"You know," Big Feather said to get his attention; "As I grew to be a man, I saw how much Chief Black Horn took this village very seriously. My son, as I sat on the high hill, his spirit came to me. He offered me important advice: he instructed me to destroy that demon golf course and take back our land, for our people. We were victorious, and we did this together."

Pale Moon smiles.

"Someone else came to me on that high hill. She is a powerful Indian spirit named Yellow Robe. She told me that you are meant to be here with us, my son; that you will always be important to this village; and that, one day, you will be chief of your own village."

Pale Moon is confused by this. He wants to respond but, instead, he stays silent to hear more.

"My son, you must find love."

Pale Moon shakes his head slightly.

Big Feather gently touches him on his shoulder. "When you find love, you will find yourself."

Before Pale Moon could respond, a little girl sits by him. She smiles at him.

"What is your name?" Pale Moon asked her sweetly.

"I am Pink Rose, daughter of Walks as a Bear and Forest Water, and young sister of Morning Blossom."

"Morning Blossom, of course," Big Feather grunted.

"What, father?" Pale Moon asked.

"*She* is the one for you."

"No, father. I don't think so."

"My sister is over there." Pink Rose points.

There she is, a woman of ethereal yet modest beauty; with a gentle face and long, straight hair. She sits in between her parents, as any single Indian woman should do. She smiles at the dancers and claps her hands.

When Pale Moon sees her, he feels everything stop around him. It is suddenly quiet—as though nothing else exists but the two of them.

"Pale Moon?" Big Feather asked a second time. He nudges him. Pale Moon responds. "Where were you?"

"What?"

"That is it, I am going to arrange a meeting," Big Feather insists. "I will meet with Walks as a Bear."

Just then, the ghost dancers emerge from a tipi to perform their dance. Pale Moon suddenly falls into an even deeper distraction when they start to perform. Their dance puts him in a trace that forces all of his feelings and thoughts to stir inside his head. He drifts off to a tranquil state of mind, and he decides at that very moment to let life take him wherever it wants. He begins to finally surrender to inner peace; he does not remember ever feeling this way, and it feels good.

He turns back to Big Feather, but he is not there. He turns again and notices that Walks as a Bear is also gone. He looks at Morning Blossom, at her delicate beauty. He then smiles to himself.

* * *

On the following day, late afternoon, Pale Moon and Morning Blossom walk along the shore together. They are attracted to each other, and between them is much excitement. They smile often and talk little, and any words that they do say are awkward, but playful.

"My father says that you are 'good medicine' for me," Pale Moon said.

"Are you unwell?" She smiles.

"I don't know."

"You don't look unwell."

"Thank you."

"I was told that you fought bravely at the golf course."

"Well, I don't really like the sport anyway."

They walk a few more steps.

"Where are you from?" she asked.

"It's sort of complicated, really."

"Why?"

"Well, I don't remember any of my past. All I remember is sitting on a bench on the boardwalk. Before that, nothing."

She mocks examining his head. "Did you bump yourself?"

"I don't think so." He looks out at the ocean. "I do have dreams of a woman and a baby girl. But, I don't know who they are." He picks up a tiny stone and throws it into the water.

"Maybe you are possessed by an evil spirit," she asked in jest.

"Well, that's what my father thinks. I would get help, but this tribe doesn't have a medicine man. Although, I think one member may be a pharmacist."

"Hissing Badger," she said.

They both laugh.

"Maybe I am good medicine for you," she said with a broad smile.

Pale Moon smiles back. He looks down and sees a small, colorful shell. He picks it up and dusts off the clinging sand.

"Here." He hands it to her.

"Thank you. So lovely."

"Like you," he said.

She looks deeply into his eyes.

"I trust you. Whatever your past is, maybe we can find it together; or, at least, maybe we can create a future of our own."

They hold hands and continue walking.

Above them and to the south, storm clouds accumulate and give the sky a burst of orange and red. The winds high above them blow increasingly strong.

* * *

After he wishes Morning Blossom a good night, Pale Moon walks to his tipi. Juicy Fruit, while listening to a small transistor radio, updates him on the path of Hurricane Ignatius. Reports say that it is heading north, but it is believed to be moving out to sea.

Pale Moon is hopeful that the reports are correct, but he can't help but have an uneasy feeling when he looks up to the sky. For the very first time, he prays to Yellow Robe.

Chapter Nine

Pale Moon tosses in his bed. He continues to dream of that woman. This time, he sees her rising from the ocean surf. She calls out to him, but he can't hear what she says.

The forceful winds slamming against his tipi wake Pale Moon. Outside, he hears the violent sounds of Hurricane Ignatius. He quickly leaves his stable shelter.

The torrent pelts with such great tenacity that the huge drops burn his skin. Although it is hard to see, Pale Moon feels the chaos all around. He hears screams, the whistling of winds, and the crackling of debris. As he shields his eyes in an attempt to see around him, he notices Forest Water.

"Pink Rose! Where are you? Pink Rose?" She holds her head in desperation, ignoring the danger surrounding her.

Morning Blossom is also calling out. Her clothes are wet and in tatters.

"Where do you think she is?" Pale Moon asked her.

"I don't know!" Morning Blossom answered. "She was with my parents, and then she screamed and ran out of the tipi. She was so scared."

Pale Moon then feels something drawing him to the surf. He turns to Morning Blossom.

"Stay with your mother and father! I want you to keep them safe!"

"Where are you going?" she asked.

"I'm not sure. But, just stay with your parents."

Morning Blossom quickly embraces him before he slips away and disappears into the deluge.

* * *

While at the surf, Pale Moon sees something floating in the ocean. Without thinking, he quickly dives in and swims toward it. He feels the powerful current tear at his body. He is besieged by great forces and begins to drown, but he doesn't panic. Rather, he senses that he is not alone.

The young woman from his dreams then appears from below. She touches his arm, and keeps him afloat. She gently and swiftly guides him to Pink Rose. With all of his might, he grabs the limp little girl and swims to shore. He then carefully lays her body on the sand.

With a few breaths into her small lungs and a few chest compressions, water propels from her mouth.

As she is coughing, Juicy Fruit appears. Using his great strength, he reaches down, picks them both up, and carefully carries them to the safety of the village.

* * *

Although the storm was severe, much of the village is still intact. None of the villagers' lives were lost.

The villagers who left for the winter months have either arrived or are on their way back to the village. All villagers have heard what happened with Pale Moon, and they are extremely delighted with his heroics.

The village reconstruction is quickly underway. First, the scattered debris and seaweed are picked up. Then, the land is leveled by rake-bearing warriors.

Some of the tipis—the stronger ones like Big Feather's and Pale Moon's—remain erect. The others are quickly raised.

Park workers toil to alleviate the flooding, restore the dunes, and affect repairs to the boardwalk. They do their work and the Indians do their work; they all effectively stay out of each other's way.

Big Feather, while on the high hill, offers thanks to the spirits of the sky and waters for sparing the lives of his people. He especially gives thanks for giving Pale Moon strength and courage.

After his prayers, he rises to his feet and walks back to the village bearing a broad smile.

* * *

Pale Moon lays on his bed resting as Juicy Fruit watches over him.

"For a white man, you are more red than white," Juicy Fruit quipped.

"I feel more tired than ever."

"Here, drink this." Juicy Fruit brings a small bowl to his mouth.

"Don't you think I drank *enough* water?"

"Just drink."

Pale Moon sips and coughs loudly.

"Wha—?" He quickly sits up.

"I made it myself. It is a special tea."

"Special?"

"It got you up, did it not?"

"Yes, I'm up, I'm up!"

Juicy Fruit changes his tone. "You know, you are a hero."

"No, I'm not."

"Yes, you are. But, let me ask you: How did you know where Pink Rose was?"

"I saw her in the water."

"How did you know to look there first?"

Pale Moon thinks. "Where would you look first?"

Just then, the tipi flap opens wide. Big Feather enters.

"My son. Are you resting well?"

"Yes, father."

"Excuse me," Juicy Fruit said. He quickly leaves the tipi.

"There will be a great feast, my son. There is so much to celebrate."

"How is Pink Rose?"

"She is very well. She is with a very grateful family."

"I'm glad."

"You rest, my son. No work for you. Just rest."

"Thank you, father."

Just as Big Feather leaves, he turns to Pale Moon.

"I love you, my son. I love you as any proud father loves his son."

"I love you, too, father."

When the flap closes, Pale Moon erupts into tears.

* * *

A news crew arrives at the village to report on the storm's aftermath. They received information in particular from a beach visitor who witnessed the rescue from the boardwalk and called the local news station with the story.

After the reporter asked a few villagers where the rescuer is, he finally locates Pale Moon recovering next to his tipi.

Pale Moon is kind and forthright as he briefly interviews him on camera. After the interview, the reporter asks him his name. He answers.

"My name is Pale Moon, son of Chief Big Feather and Little Mouth; brother of Four Winds."

* * *

The villagers honor Pale Moon in a ceremony that outdoes the last one. All are in attendance to celebrate and offer thanks for surviving the violent storm. They feast, they dance, and they chant.

Pink Rose sits on Pale Moon's lap in the company of their families. They are adorned in colorful ceremonial clothes as they smile and clap their hands to the tribal music. Pink Rose turns to

Pale Moon. She kisses him on the cheek and hugs him.

On the boardwalk, another news crew arrives to cover the event. The reporter musters the courage to walk into the village and up to where Pale Moon sits.

"Sir, are you Pale Moon?" the reporter asked.

"Yes," he answered almost reluctantly. "Who are you?"

"I am a reporter from LI-Nine. Would you mind if I asked you a few questions about the rescue of a little girl?"

"Oh, but I was already interviewed."

"It will only be for a minute, promise."

Pale Moon looks to Big Feather.

"It is up to you, my son."

"Yes," Pale Moon answered.

They walk together to the boardwalk where the crew awaits. With the village in the background, the reporter interviews.

"I'm here at Jones Beach with Indian reenactor, Pale Moon—the man who saved a little girl from drowning during Hurricane Ignatius. Sir, how does it feel to be a hero?"

"Well, I wouldn't call myself a hero. Any Algonquin Indian would have done what I did."

"You are Algonquin."

"Yes, I am."

"I see, part Indian."

"No, I am all Indian," he insists. "My father and my mother are Indians. My brother is an Indian. This is my home. I am loved here."

"You certainly are." The reporter turns to the camera. "This is Chris Lodge, LI-Nine News, reporting from Jones Beach."

"Thank you, Pale Moon. That was great."

Pale Moon nods and raises his hand.

The cameraman holds back a laugh.

Chapter Ten

News breaks that the Council of Elders of the Shinnecock Nation was experienceing a leadership issue. They learned that Benjamin Archer was planning a secret deal with Ronald Drake outside of the Council's knowledge and approval.

Archer attempted to give away much of the Nation's beach property rights in an arrangement that would be regarded as double-dipping on the part of Drake Casino Resorts because this deal was contrived outside of the Council's purview.

Upon completion of the Council's full investigation, it concluded that the deal involved the creation of a casino and hotel that would dominate the entire beach park of Jones Beach.

The secret plan included the dismantling of the Indian village in favor or a profit-gaining miniature golf course and other attractions and businesses. The plan also included the driving out of existing businesses—including Amir's shop—in favor of Indian-owned and run businesses to be selected by

Archer himself. It was believed that the prospective new businesses may need to arrange a specific contract with Archer prior to establishing themselves at the beach park.

The Council first became suspicious when the village was removed and the miniature golf course was installed. When the village land was reacquired by Chief Big Feather, the Council intervened with authorities to prevent the villagers from being removed a second time.

After careful consideration by the Council of Elders, Archer is forced to immediately resign from office. They determined that he engaged in willful neglect of duty, corruption in office, unethical behavior, misconduct in the affairs of the Shinnecock Nation, and conduct unbecoming of a tribal official. His swift resignation, as well as the stripping of his wealth that he accumulated as a result of his unsanctioned activities, serves as part of a plea deal that protects him from criminal liability. Some critics of the Council say that their decision is way too lenient, while others believe the shame inflicted on Archer is enough punishment. Immediately after the Council's decision, Archer disappeared somewhere out west and into obscurity.

Out of respect for Big Feather, as a gesture of good faith, and due to the negative publicity surrounding the incident, the Council votes to allow special rights and privileges to be granted to the village, and approves for the village land to be expanded to the west. They dispatch an Indian work crew from the reservation in Suffolk County to demolish the neighboring shuffleboard and paddle tennis courts up to a small gazebo for those lands to be used by the villagers.

* * *

It is not long before the newly-expanded village is well on its way to becoming a complete community.

Some of the acquired property has been set aside for farming for the upcoming warmer months, while construction is underway for additional tipis, a fish-curing hut, and a few artisan huts for manufacturing pottery, baskets, clothing, and blankets. A classroom and a visitor's center are also in the making, while a small stable is also being constructed after commitments were made for the community to receive two additional horses.

Pale Moon walks among the workers, helping wherever he can. He is approached by an excited Juicy Fruit.

"Best of all, Pale Moon, I no longer need to share a tipi with Leaping Frog," he said. "He is noisy when he sleeps."

Pale Moon smiles. "Maybe he can say the same for you, my friend." He reaches high up to pat him on the shoulder.

In the distance, Pale Moon sees a figure drawing closer. He squints his eyes slightly, and then sees that it is Amir. Amir is so awestruck by all the construction that he doesn't see Pale Moon until they are a short distance away.

"Amir."

"Tahmin. How are you?"

"I'm fine. How are you? How is your family?"

"Fine. We are all fine. Hey, I see you have new clothes—you are an Indian now. And, your hair and beard are trimmed; you look much cleaner. What I mean is that it looks like you found yourself. I am so glad for you."

"I'm getting there," Pale Moon said with a tired smile.

"What I mean to say is that I am sorry about what has happened between us."

"There is no need to be sorry. You were right; you have a family to support."

"Yes, Tahmin, but you were my friend, and I hope that we can be friends again."

"Amir, you've never stopped being my friend."

The men embrace.

"Well, I would offer you your old room back, but I see that you have a home here. You are always welcome to visit me and my family."

"Thank you, Amir. You, too." Pale Moon smiles. "I do miss your wife's cooking."

"No, you do not."

"Yes, I do."

"It gave you gas."

"Yeah, it did."

"It gives me gas all the time."

Both men laugh.

"When the village re-opens in the spring, you should bring your daughters. It should be a lot of fun for them."

"I will."

Leaping Frog walks by.

"I will have my own tipi, Pale Moon. I am so happy. Juicy Fruit snores so loud."

"Pale Moon?" Amir asked.

"Yes, that's what they call me."

Amir thinks for a moment and smiles.

"This name suits you," he said.

FRANCIS JOHN BALDUCCI

Chapter Eleven

As one of the several news stories covering Hurricane Ignatius, Pale Moon's face is transmitted on two of the island's top news channels.

"His name? Pale Moon. His story is a hero's story," a reporter said as a voice over in one news story. *"But, who is this shy, modest Indian re-enactor of the Jones Beach Indian attraction? We caught up to him in this exclusive interview."*

"My name is Pale Moon. I am an Algonquin Indian." He gestured to his tipi. *"This is my home."*

"You are a hero," the reporter said off camera.

"I am just a man, nothing more. I put on my pants the same way as any other man. Except, my pants were made by Falcon Eyes. She lives in the tipi right over there." He points.

"But, you saved a little girl from drowning. I think that makes you a hero."

"I only did what anyone would have done. Now, please leave me alone."

Pale Moon hurries off camera. The reporter quickly steps into frame.

"Dan Abernacky, LITV-Three News."

* * *

In a quite stylish home near the north shore of Long Island, Pale Moon's face appears on a tall television screen. The home's occupant—a clean-cut, middle-aged man—sees the face and quickly picks up the remote control to raise the volume.

"He's alive?" he said. He listens intensely.

"...Jones Beach Indian attraction..."

"...I am an Algonquin Indian..."

"He's alive!"

The man stumbles as he quickly puts on his pants. He grabs his car keys and then leaps out the door.

* * *

Big Feather prays atop the high hill. He foresees a struggle involving Pale Moon. He fears the man's very life may be threatened. He focuses deeper to see what the danger may be, but nothing clear materializes.

After a moment, he sees another vision. It consists of a young woman rising from the ocean. Her image is ghostly yet clear as she gently approaches him.

As she then stands before him, she tries to communicate with Big Feather, but he doesn't fully understand her. So, he speaks to her.

"Who are you, my child?"

"Diane," she answered in a faint voice.

"Are you a goddess of the sea?"

"Tell Brian that I will not leave until he finds himself."

"Who is Brian?"

The image vanishes into the wind before he receives an answer. Big Feather closes his eyes in order to summon her back. But, he is unsuccessful.

"I know no Brian," he said to himself.

* * *

Pale Moon sits in his tipi after having a lunch of local venison. He marvels over a gift that he received from Forest Water. It's a new chest plate she fashioned from several beads and shells. The design is intricate and beautifully colored. He puts it on and places both fists on his hips. He sports a proud face and takes a deep breath.

"Are you inside, my son?"

"Yes, father. Please enter."

Big Feather enters.

"Well, I see that you are ready for another battle," Big Feather said with a smile.

"Yeah," Pale Moon responded as he removes the garment.

Big Feather sits next to him.

"Something troubles me, my son."

"What, father?"

"As I prayed on the high hill, the spirit of a young, white woman appeared to me from the waters.

She was very beautiful and bold. Do you know of her?"

"No, father. But, I do have dreams from time to time of a woman rising up. Sometimes there is fire around her. I think I saw her in the ocean during the great storm when I was with Pink Rose."

"Is the name Diane familiar to you?"

"No." Pale Moon thinks more. "No, not at all."

"Are you certain?"

"Yes, I don't know anyone with that name."

"Maybe she is a goddess sent here to protect you. You say you saw her in the waters when you saved Pink Rose?"

"Well, I didn't really *see* her. I think my mind was playing tricks with me."

"Perhaps you are right."

Both men sit quietly for a moment.

"My son, will you go to the high hill with me where we will pray together?"

"Yes, father."

"Will you go now?"

"Now?"

"Yes, now."

"All right, father. Do I need to bring anything with me?"

"An open heart."

Both men leave the tipi and walk toward the hill. Pale Moon is not fully aware of or confident in what they will accomplish. But, he does know that he should never question his chief. Big Feather is concerned that there may be an evil spirit lurking about, and he is eager to find answers.

* * *

Morning Blossom sits in her parents' tipi with Forest Water. The mother sits behind her daughter carefully combing the young woman's hair with long gentle strokes. Morning Blossom's eyes are closed.

"You have my mother's hair," Forest Water said. "So strong and thick."

Both women remain silent for a few moments.

"What do you think of Pale Moon?" Forest Water asked.

Morning Blossom opens her eyes. "What do *you* think of him?"

"Well, I am grateful he is with us. He risked his own life to save Pink Rose. I think that makes him family." She pauses. "Tell me what *you* think of him."

Just as Morning Blossom is about to answer, Walks as a Bear enters the tipi.

"I have fish," he said. He throws a log on the fire.

"Father, what do you think of Pale Moon?"

"I owe him my life."

"Do you owe him your daughter?" Forest Water asked.

"Which one?" Walks as a Bear said with a puzzled look.

"Be serious," Forest Water said.

"I don't know. He is a white man."

"He is a *good* man," Morning Blossom said.

"He is a good man—a very good man. There are good white men and bad red men. I wish him to be good and red, but this is not so."

"But I care for him," Morning Blossom said.

"Bear," Forest Water interrupts; "is it more important for the man to be conveniently red or for the man to be the one she wants?"

"Both. Why not both," he answered.

"Sometimes, my dear husband, it does not happen that way. Besides, Chief Big Feather says Pale Moon is one of us, in spirit."

Walks as a Bear turns to Morning Blossom. "How do you feel about this white man? How does he feel about you? Tell me, child!"

Morning Blossom breaks down into tears and storms out of the tipi.

"You have been out in the sun too long, husband."

"I only want what is best for her."

"You want what is best for you," Forest Water said with tears in her eyes.

"I want what is best for our people."

* * *

On the high hill, the Pale Moon and Big Feather sit with their legs crossed facing each other.

Big Feather meditates so deeply that he undergoes a self-induced trance. In his mind, he sees many of the visions that Pale Moon has witnessed for so long; these visions come and they go. He attempts to conjure them by making demands for them to appear. He grows impatient to communicate with whatever lies within the dark abyss. He becomes increasingly demanding and, still, he doesn't receive any response. His is determined to rid Pale Moon of his visions for good. He also attempts to remove any residual pain of his former self.

Pale Moon sits still. Even though he tries very hard to fall into a meditative state, he is unsuccessful. As he thinks back, all he can think about are all of his encounters and experiences starting with that one lonely day on a boardwalk bench.

He thinks of his time in the ocean nearly drowning, and that he somehow found Pink Rose and brought her to shore. "How could I have saved her?" he thought.

He then thinks of Morning Blossom. He thinks of her face and her form. Pale Moon wonders how a woman could be so beautiful. Then, the vision of the young woman returns. She takes him by the hand and pulls him toward her. He feels her hand feel hotter and hotter with every passing moment. He tries to break away, but he cannot; she holds on so tightly. She then bursts into flames and screams. The fire engulfs her and moves up her arm to where she is holding Pale Moon. He cries out.

"Father, help me!"

"I am here my son! Turn to me!"

Big Feather, looking like a grand, young Indian warrior in spectacular clothes and war paint on his face, calls to Pale Moon.

"Take my hand, my son!"

Pale Moon takes Big Feather's hand. Just before the fire travels up to Pale Moon's other hand, the fiery woman releases him.

Both men wake from their trance. Pale Moon quickly embraces the chief.

"It is all right, my son. I don't think she will be back. I think I scared her away."

"I hope so, father."

Big Feather rises with him.

"Let's go home, my son," he said.

They begin to descend from the hill.

"Little Mouth is making opossum stew just for you."

The chief is uncertain if he is successful at eliminating Pale Moon's attacks. But, he is hopeful.

"Opossum stew, just for me?"

As they near the village, they see Morning Blossom.

"Father, would it be all right if I eat later?"

"Yes, my son." Big Feather turns to face him. "All the blessings in the world cannot compare to the love of one woman." He smiles and walks off.

As Pale Moon sees him walk away, Morning Blossom approaches.

"I want to talk," she said.

"Okay."

"I wish to walk away from the village."

She walks off leaving Pale Moon. He shrugs his shoulders and follows her.

* * *

"Did I do something wrong?" Pale Moon asked.

"It is not you," she answered.

"That's a relief."

"It is my father—it is me."

"That's a lot of people." He grins.

"I am being serious!"

"Okay, I'm sorry. What is wrong?"

She stops walking and takes a deep breath. "How do you feel about me?"

"Why do you need to know right now?"

"Please answer me."

Pale Moon looks out to the ocean. "Well, I think you are the most amazing woman that I've ever met. I think of you all the time: before I close my eyes when I sleep, I think of your face; and when I wake, your face is still in my mind."

When Pale Moon looks back at Morning Blossom's face, she is in tears.

"Why are you crying?" he asked.

"Because my father is being so difficult."

"Why?"

"Because you are a white man."

"But, I'm *not* a white man—not anymore."

She looks away.

"Do you love me?" he asked.

"Yes, I do. I loved you at first sight, and I will love you forever. But, I do not think my father will give us his blessing."

"Let's run away together." He takes her hands.

"I cannot. It is not the Algonquin way."

"Then, I'll just have a talk with Walks as a Bear. My father says that we will celebrate Native Americans' Day this year. I'll speak with him then. I'll reason with him."

"I am also worried about the village accepting us. When most of them return in the spring, they may be confused."

"Morning Blossom, we have to give our fellow Indians a lot more credit. They are all intelligent people."

"Leaping Frog is intelligent?"

"Well..."

"Sleeping Elk is intelligent?"

"Well, most of our fellow Indians are intelligent. Besides, they know what love is, and they love us. They know I love you."

Morning Blossom folds into Pale Moon's arms. They look deeply into each other's eyes as their lips collide in a passionate kiss. They then walk off around the high hill while holding hands.

* * *

"I'm looking for a man about six feet tall, long hair and a beard," the clean-cut, middle-aged man said while he shows a photograph to a park worker on the boardwalk. "He hangs out here around the Indian attraction."

"Nope, never seen him," the park worker said.

"Okay, thanks."

He sees another man who appears to be a park official. He walks up to him and shows him the photograph.

"Have you seen him?"

"I don't know," the official said.

"He's wearing a beard and long hair now."

"Hmm, he does look a little familiar."

"Here, let me give you this." The man hands him a business card. "My name is Steve. If you see him, please give me a call right away."

"No problem."

Steve is apprehensive to enter the Indian village. So, he continues to walk up and down the boardwalk, from the east bathhouse to the west bathhouse.

He thinks he sees the man in the photograph walking away from him. He runs up behind him and touches him of the shoulder. The man turns around.

"Oh, I'm sorry," Steve said. "I thought you were someone else."

After a few hours, Steve decides to leave the beach park and return home. He is uncertain whether or not to contact the authorities. But, he does know that he needs to visit the beach park again soon and continue his search for him.

FRANCIS JOHN BALDUCCI

Chapter Twelve

Steve conducts another search for the man at Jones Beach—his fourth of such kind.

He is becoming increasingly frustrated that he can't find this man. He has even asked the few people around if they have seen a man named Pale Moon. But, these people offer him no help.

Steve also begins to question whether or not his eyes may have fooled him—that, perhaps, the man interviewed on the television is really not the man he thinks he is.

Tired, he stares up at the brick tower beyond a grassy plaza. If this man is indeed around, he worries about him, where he may be, and whether or not he is safe. As desperate that Steve is to find answers, he also wonders if this may all be a figment of his imagination and a total waste of his time. But, he decides to stay at the beach park just a little while longer. Maybe he should enter the Indian village; maybe he should keep watching the village from the boardwalk. Just then, a yawn escapes from his mouth.

While the sun disappears behind Steve, he watches the park workers take down the American flag at the park's main flag mast. He considers that it is time to go. As he turns to leave, he sees Pale Moon standing at attention rendering a salute to the flag being slowly lowered into the workers' hands.

"Brian?" Steve said.

Pale Moon looks at him. "Excuse me?"

"Brian, it's me."

"Me, who?"

"Steve, your kid brother." He quickly embraces him and holds on tightly. "I thought you were dead—we all did?"

Pale Moon allows this man to hold him. He is a bit shocked.

"You must have me confused with someone else. I don't know you."

Steve lets him go and takes a step back. He looks him directly in his eyes.

"Brian, don't you remember me? Don't you remember anything? Tell me, Brian!"

"Why do you keep calling me Brian?"

"It's your name, Brian—Brian Nance."

"That is not my name. That was never my name. My name is Pale Moon. I am an Algonquin Indian and I live here in the village."

"No, you are Brian Nance. You are an anthropology professor. You lived in Massapequa Park. You was a volunteer firefighter. You left us over a year ago. And, now, I'm here to take you home."

"I am home! Leave me alone!"

"Your wife, Brian. Do you remember your wife?"

"I don't have a wife."

"I was the best man at your wedding."

"I'm telling you that I have no wife."

"You did, Brian. You did and now she is dead. She died. Do you remember that? Do you remember Diane?"

"Get away from me!"

"And, your daughter? Do you remember her? Do you remember your daughter, Alexandra?"

"I said get away from me?" Pale Moon tries to walk away, but Steve keeps up with him.

"Well, she's dead, too. Don't you remember?"

"You're insane! I know none of these people. Why are you telling me they are dead? Go away!"

"They were your wife and daughter. They died when a drunk driver sideswiped her car on the Southern Parkway."

"I don't know any of this."

"You had them cremated. We had a ceremony. We chartered a boat to scatter their ashes in the ocean—out there." Steve points toward the water. "Don't you remember?"

"No, please!"

"Why did you run away, Brian? You didn't have to do that? We thought you were dead. The police found your car nearby on the side of the parkway. There was no trace of you. So, we thought you drowned yourself in the ocean."

"Are you crazy? I'm telling you I don't know you. I don't know who these people are that you speak of. I am Pale Moon. I am the son of Big Feather and Little Mouth, and the brother of Four

Winds. I am an Algonquin Indian, I live here at Jones Beach, and this is the only home that I have ever known."

Steve is stunned and stops following Pale Moon. He tries to find more words to say, but his lips remain still.

Pale Moon turns to him.

"Whoever you are, you are mentally ill; and I feel very sorry for you."

Pale Moon quickly walks off.

"But, Brian. I love you! There are people that love you. Please come..."

Steve thinks for a moment. He is convinced that his brother is suffering from some sort of mental trauma. He believes that his brother blocked out the horror that has happened to him and decided— whether he knows it or not—to live in an alternate reality. He is deeply concerned for him, and he is afraid that he will never get his brother back.

* * *

Steve is in his home. He is in deep thought as he walks around from room to room. He is glad that his brother is alive and looking well. However, he also grasps the fact that his brother is not entirely himself. He struggles with what to do next.

He thinks of going back to the beach park to try to convince him of the truth. He also thinks that another destructive exchange may make matters far worse. He also considers that his behavior may be destructive and, possibly, life threatening. He is uncertain if he may do something completely irrational or dangerous.

He sits for a moment and decides to pick up the phone and make a call.

"Hello, Pilgrim Psychiatric Center?   Doctor Pendleton, please... Thank you. Hello, doctor. This is Steve Nance again—we spoke last week. I am calling to have my brother committed... Yes, I know exactly where he is. Yes, I do believe that he's a danger to himself and to others..."

Chapter Thirteen

On two occasions, the authorities came close to finding Pale Moon. On one sunny afternoon, however, they locate him as he returns to the village after spear fishing with Sleeping Elk. The authorities simply walk into the village.

These men consist of a casually-dressed facility administrator accompanied by two heavy-set clinical technicians dressed entirely in white with black bow ties and two uniformed police officers. The administrator approaches Pale Moon and shows him a signed, official document.

"Sir, we have a court order to take you with us," the administrator said. "It is for your own good. We may take you by force, if necessary. Don't make us put you in restraints."

One police officer speaks to Pale Moon and Leaping Frog with an authoritative tone.

"Gentlemen, please put down your spears."

Pale Moon's spear, with several fish pierced on it, drops to the ground. Sleeping Elk, however, still holds his spear. The officer speaks again.

"Sir, I'm ordering you to drop the spear."

Pale Moon turns to Sleeping Elk. "Let it go."

Juicy Fruit walks to where the men are standing. He looks at the clinical technicians.

"I can break both of you in half," he said.

Pale Moon looks at him. "No, my friend. We will not have that." He turns to the men. "There is no need for force; I will come with you peacefully."

Just then, Big Feather emerges from his tipi with Little Mouth. Pale Moon looks at them. As their eyes meet, a deep sadness overcomes their faces.

While Pale Moon remains in Indian clothes, the technicians come to either side of him with both police officers behind. The administrator gestures for all the men to follow him toward the boardwalk.

Morning Blossom sees Pale Moon being taken away. She calls out to him, but Pale Moon can't bear to turn around to see her.

By the time the men enter the boardwalk and in the direction of a parking lot, the remaining villagers merely stand around, stunned. Sleeping Elk, feeling helpless, begins to cry. Juicy Fruit makes an attempt to calm him. Leaping Frog shrieks a battle cry that goes unanswered by the fellow villagers.

Four Winds appears from his tipi. He shouts at the men.

"Where are you taking my brother?"

Pale Moon is carefully placed in a white van. When he sits in the seat, he closes his eyes for a moment. The van starts, and it drives away on the Wantagh Parkway.

During the ride, Pale Moon looks out of the window. He has not seen the world outside the beach park for a long time; he does not recognize anything he sees.

In twenty minutes, he arrives at the Pilgrim Psychiatric Center in the town of Brentwood.

After the van enters the facility grounds, the police escort leaves. Pale Moon is walked into Building 82—a tall, brick edifice. He is taken into an elevator going up. He is then moved down a long corridor to the intensive treatment unit. While he passes a curved archway of the isolated ward, he is maneuvered around other patients. One patient raises one hand in a greeting gesture.

"How," he said in a deep voice.

* * *

In a small, isolated examination room, Pale Moon, while still wearing his Indian clothing, sits on an aluminum chair facing an empty, cushioned chair and a simple desk. He looks around the room and sees no other furniture. There is a window, but the glass is entirely translucent. No thoughts enter his mind specifically; he has no expectation of what is going to happen to him. He peers over the desktop to see only a notepad. After a moment, the door behind him swings open, and a man dressed in a well-cut, formal suit enters the room. He has a few newspapers tucked under his arm. He quickly puts the papers down, sits behind the desk, and removes a gold pen from his jacket as he takes the notepad in his hand.

"Hello, Brian. My name is Doctor Charles Pendleton. I am a psychiatrist."

"Hello, my name is Pale Moon."

"Well, of course it is. I am here to conduct a psychological analysis of you. Do you understand?"

Pale Moon nods slightly but with little understanding of the question.

"Good. Now, let me start by asking you why you think your name is Pale Moon."

"Because it is Pale Moon. My name is also Tahmin. It is Persian. It means 'brave'."

"Is that so."

"I am known by different names to different people."

"Really?" He scribbles in the notepad.

"I'm sure that not all people call you Doctor Pendleton. Some people call you Charles. Some people call you Charlie."

"That's true. But..."

"So, I am a man of different names, nothing more."

"Do you know when you were born?"

Pale Moon thinks for a moment. "I arrived on a bench on the boardwalk."

The doctor scribbles. "Do you know how old you are?"

"Pale Moon shakes his head. "I am an adult."

"Well, what if I told you that you are thirty-six years old?"

"I suppose you would be correct."

"All right. Now, tell me about your family."

"Big Feather is my father. He is a great chief and the powerful leader of our people."

The doctor scribbles. "And your mother?"

"Little Mouth is a loving and caring mother."

"She cared for you as a baby and as you grew up to be a man."

Pale Moon thinks. "No, she adopted me."

"At thirty-five years old? At thirty-six? When did she adopt you?"

"She is the only mother that I have ever known."

The doctor scribbles. "And, what about your brother?"

"Four Winds is a brave and wise younger brother."

"Isn't your younger brother named Steve?"

"I know who you speak of, but I don't know this man. I never knew this man. I think he is crazy."

"Brian..."

"Please, stop calling me Brian!"

"Okay, let's go somewhere else. Tell me about some of your friends." The doctor scratches his head.

"I have known Amir for over a year. He is a shopkeeper on the boardwalk. He took me in, fed me, and introduced me to his family."

"So, you know them well."

"Yes, I do. I love them."

The doctor scratches his chin.

"Are you married?"

"No, I am not. Not yet."

"Not yet?"

"I don't know if her father will have me. I don't think he will."

"What if I told you that he already said it's okay?"

"You mean Walks as a Bear gave his blessing?"

"Who's Walks as a Bear?"

"He is her father."

"The father of whom?"

"My true love—my only love."

"What if I told you that you were already married, and that your wife died in a car crash, and that her name was Diane?"

"No, my love is alive, and her name is Morning Blossom."

The doctor scribbles. "Sir, do you experience hallucinations, visions, or lucid dreams?"

"I often dream of a young woman. I am not certain if I know her. She is beautiful, but something horrible happens to her. I see flames, and I hear screaming."

"I see," the doctor said as he writes. "Anything else?"

"I also see a child—a toddler girl. She is also screaming. Flames are everywhere."

"Your daughter?"

"I have no children."

"I see, well, let's explore something else. The news story on you has made you a bit of a sensation."

"I don't know anything about that."

"Oh, sure. You made all the papers." The doctor opens the newspapers and spreads them on the desk. "See?"

Pale Moon gazes over the pages with a blank look.

"It feels good to be a hero, huh?" the doctor asked.

"I don't know."

"Oh, sure. It's a great feeling."

"I don't know. I just had to save Pink Rose."

"Of course you did. She was drowning."

"Yes, she was."

"How did you know she was drowning? I mean, she could have been anywhere during that storm. Did you see her walk into the ocean?"

"No, I just knew where she was."

"But, how did you know where she was?"

"I was drawn to her."

"You were drawn to her, how?"

"I don't know."

"Could it be that you brought her there?"

"What?"

"Could it be that you brought her into the ocean with you?"

"Why would I do that?"

"Why don't you tell me."

"I don't know what you mean."

"Could it be that you took the little girl into the ocean to make it appear to everyone that you rescued her?"

"I don't know what you mean."

"You took the little girl into the ocean so that you could look like a big hero to the Indians, and so that they would accept you, right?"

"That's not true!"

"You needed to belong."

"*No!* I had to save her!"

"Did someone see you jump into the ocean?"

"I don't know."

"Did someone see you take her out?"

"There was someone in the water with us."

"Who?"

"I don't know. It was that young woman from my dreams that I already told you about."

"She was in the water with you."

"I think so. I felt her."

"I see." The doctor writes in the notebook.

A moment passes. Pale Moon looks down at his hands. He glances a few times at the newspapers. Then, he looks at the doctor.

"Doctor Pendleton, when do I get to go home? When will I be with my family again?"

The doctor continues to write. He answers him without looking up.

"Well, we're just going to run a few more tests. So, I'd like you to be a little patient with us."

Pale Moon looks back down at his hands.

The doctor stands with the notepad and newspapers. "I'll see you again in a few days. Please cooperate with the staff. They are here to help you."

Pale Moon nods as the doctor leaves. A moment later the technicians enter the room to take him.

As Pale Moon is escorted down a corridor lined with fellow patients, one speaks to him in a clear and direct voice.

"Don't cry, chief. If you do, they will hurt you more." She then giggles.

* * *

The following day, Steve enters the ward and arrives at Pale Moon's room. He's carrying an item in a small paper bag.

He sees Pale Moon sitting up in his bed wearing a hospital gown. A breakfast tray sits on a small table near the bed. No food was eaten. Steve clears his throat and speaks.

"Hey, how ya' feelin'?"

Pale Moon looks up at him. He looks tired.

"Brian, I thought I'd stop by to see if you need anything."

Pale Moon doesn't respond.

"You know, the sooner you get better, the sooner you get to come home with me."

Pale Moon continues to look at him.

"Hey, I got you something I know you love."

Steve opens the paper bag and reveals a package of Twinkies cakes.

"Good? These are your favorites. I figure you haven't had these in a long time. Here."

Steve hands the cakes to him, but Pale Moon doesn't take them.

"Okay, well, I'll just put them here." He puts the cakes on the tray. "Maybe you'll have them later."

Pale Moon keeps looking at him, never changing his expression.

"Okay, I'm going to see the doctor now. I'm sure he's got great things to tell me. And then, I'll see you later this week." Steve smiles at him as he leaves, but he still doesn't receive a response of any kind.

After he leaves, Pale Moon looks at the cakes and thinks. Then, a grimaced expression overcomes his face.

* * *

"Mister Nance, I examined your brother carefully, and I think his condition is pretty serious. I'll continue to evaluate him, but, it's not like he's going to be released anytime soon."

"What do you mean? What's wrong?"

The doctor looks down at an open file on his desk.

"Based on my initial tests, your brother suffers from schizophrenia, perhaps of the paranoid classification."

"What, how so?"

Well, your brother fails to recognize reality as we know it; he has false beliefs and his thinking is drastically unclear and confused. He has socially isolated himself from his real life and he's adopted an entirely new identity. He also suffers from debilitating hallucinations."

"Oh, my!"

"It's even worse than that, I'm afraid: he also suffers from a serious case of psychogenic amnesia, specifically, a form of repressed-memory retrograde amnesia brought on due to the trauma of losing his wife and daughter. The effects consist of long-term memory loss and impairment. Simply put, after their deaths, Brian went into deep shock. He drove to Jones Beach and simply stayed. It was there where his mental illness crept in. Is it true that he took his family to Jones Beach often?"

"Yes, they went there a lot."

"I suppose he was familiar with the Indian attraction."

"Yeah, they told me that it was an interesting exhibit."

"I see. Well, I am also diagnosing Brian with dissociative identity disorder with the Indian personality dominating his true identity. I must say, your brother is a rare case. I believe he will need to be committed indefinitely."

"I don't believe this."

"Mister Nance, I'm sorry. His road to recovery will be very long and extremely rough. Your strength and involvement will be most needed to help Brian regain his life back. Right now, I have him on thirty milligrams of loxapine. I may need to increase this dose in order to achieve the desired effect."

"So, he'll be drugged up for much of the time."

"Well, I wouldn't quite put in that way, but, yes. But, ultimately, the medication will help bring about some improvement over time. I'll keep you updated."

"Thank you, doctor."

Steve leaves the doctor's office and walks down the hall to the elevator. Once inside, he breaks down in tears.

* * *

At the village, there is no word of Pale Moon's condition, but they do have an idea of his whereabouts. When the white van pulled out of the parking lot, Four Wings followed it on a motorbike. Upon his return to the village, he reports that Pale Moon was brought into a building complex.

"The white man has taken Pale Moon away to a soldier fort—a huge, brick beast."

The villagers are uncertain about what to do. All are deeply sad and worried about Pale Moon.

Big Feather, with very few options as a chief, dispatched an Indian envoy consisting of Gray Smoke and Slow River to Pilgrim Psychiatric Center, but both of them were turned away at the front door. Now, all that Big Feather does is pray on the high hill. He refuses to eat.

Little Mouth can be heard in a Pale Moon's tipi crying aloud. She refuses to come out until her son safely returns home.

Juicy Fruit and Leaping Frog gather together with Four Winds and Red Leaf. They express anger for the white men that took their brother. Sleeping Elk, who now joins them, attempts to conjure up evil spirits to attack the captors so that Pale Moon could break free and come home.

Morning Blossom is with her family. She tries hard to stay strong and show a brave face so that those around her wouldn't worry about her so much. But, she is not entirely successful.

"I am torn up inside!" Walks as a Bear said. He pounds his fists on the ground.

"Maybe, father, I can talk to the white men," Pink Rose said. "I will tell them how special Pale Moon is. They will release him if I just tell them. They must."

Forest Water holds Pink Rose close and kisses her on the forehead.

* * *

Pale Moon undergoes extensive tests and several brain scans. Although the brain scans reveal that his brain's cranial size is normal, the test results show that he is in no way closer to realizing his true identity.

Far worse than this, he begins to feel the effects of the medication. He is dazed most of the time, his vision is blurred, and his speech is slurred. He is lethargic in his walk and his movements, and the few times he allows himself to eat, he accomplishes the task very slowly.

In a patient community room, Pale Moon sits by himself at a table. In front of him is a checkers set with the pieces chaotically arranged. He stares at these pieces with little thought of what to do with them. He slowly moves a red piece. He then slowly moves a black piece in the same direction that he moved the red piece. He goes back to staring at the pieces.

"Hey! Whatcha doin'?" a male patient asked him as he walks by.

Pale Moon slowly looks up.

"Playin' checkers? Oh, I like that game. Here..." The patient sits down in the opposing chair and properly arranges the pieces on the board.

"Okay, pal!" the patient said. "Let's play! You go first."

Pale Moon goes back to staring at the pieces. Moments pass. The patient looks at him and the pieces and becomes impatient.

"What's wrong?" the patient asked. "Don't cha know how to play?"

Pale Moon doesn't answer. He just keeps staring at the pieces.

"Awright!" the patient said abruptly; "I'll go first."

The patient moves one. Pale Moon continues to stare down at the pieces. A few moments go by. The patient gets agitated.

"C'mon! Move one! Move *any* one!"

Pale Moon looks at him with a blank expression.

"Oh, Christ!" The patient moves a piece for him.

"There," he said. "Now I'll move." The man moves one of his pieces.

Pale Moon looks down at the pieces.

"C'mon! Move one!" he said.

Pale Moon slowly moves one of the man's pieces.

"No!—*No!* What's wrong with you? You moved one of *my* pieces!!"

A technician sees the patient stand and throw a checker piece in Pale Moon's face. He quickly intervenes and whisks Pale Moon away back to his room.

"You're not supposed to move one of *my* pieces!!" he screamed as Pale Moon was taken out of the room. "Are you *crazy* or somethin'? That hippy freak moved one of *my* pieces!!"

After Pale Moon is carefully propped up in his bed, the technician leaves and closes the door. While he sits there, a feeling of hopelessness and fear overcomes him. He thinks of Morning Blossom in an attempt relax his mind but, rather than calm him down, the thought of her only conjures up feelings of loss and loneliness and a deep belief that he will never see her again nor hold her in his arms. He remembers how close he came to freezing to death on a frigid boardwalk bench. He feels like he is back there, drawing his final breaths, dying.

* * *

Doctor Pendleton, while in his office, notes in Brian Nance's folder that his patient is not showing much progress and that he may even be deteriorating—becoming neither Brian Nance nor Pale Moon.

He is not responding well to loxapine, even at an increased dose to sixty milligrams. So, the doctor decides to administer twenty-five milligrams of clozapine. He plans on gradually increasing the dose to fifty milligrams by the end of the week.

It is still too early in his patient's treatments to give up all hope. So, the doctor decides on other methods.

He tells the nurse that he needs to schedule some sessions of electroconvulsive therapy starting next week.

* * *

Sitting on a tray on Pale Moon's bed is bottled nourishment and linen napkins. With her able fingers, the care attendant maneuvers the straw in this bottle to ensure that the tip reaches the patient's lips. When Pale Moon draws the final gulp of fluid, she removes the straw. She then lifts the tray and places it on a small table next to the bed.

Moments after finishing his lunch, his pillows behind him are removed, and he is lowered onto his side so that his soiled clothes may be changed. Afterwards, he is gently lowered into a napping position. Courtesy of the severe medication, it is not long before he slips into unconsciousness. For the most part, the world around him no longer exists.

Later that afternoon, after his nap, Pale Moon is administered more medication. He is left alone sitting up in bed. He exists in a deep stupor.

After a few minutes, an attendant wearing a surgical mask and hospital scrubs enters the room. The attendant whispers in his ear.

"Tahmin?"

The attendant removes his mask revealing his identity.

Pale Moon looks at this man's face. A smile slowly forms on his dry lips. Pale Moon speaks for the first time in weeks in a weak, shallow voice.

"Amir."

"Yes, we've come to take you home."

Just then, Juicy Fruit and Leaping Frog quickly enter the room. They realize they have to get him out quickly before they are discovered by the technicians. Amir and Leaping Frog attempt to lift Pale Moon to his feet, but his body is way too limp for him to stand on his own.

"How do we take him?" Leaping Frog asked. "I know, Juicy Fruit can lift that large, marble sink and crash it through a window. Then, we'll escape outside and run over the grassy hill."

"But, we are on the eleventh floor," Juicy Fruit said. "I have a better plan: Leaping Frog, change clothes with Pale Moon and get in his bed and cover yourself with the sheets. I'll carry Pale Moon upright out of this place and to the elevator. Red Leaf is out there doing her best. So, let's hurry!"

To further disguise Pale Moon, Amir transfers some of Leaping Frog's war paint onto Pale Moon's face with his finger. By appearance, Pale Moon is an Indian again.

With Leaping Frog in bed, and Juicy Fruit and Amir standing alongside Pale Moon somewhat propping him to his feet, they look at each other.

"Leaping Frog, cover up!" Juicy Fruit ordered. He turns to Amir. "Ready?"

"Ready," Amir responded.

They slowly and carefully peek out the door and see that all is clear. The three leave the room and make their way down a long wall where they stop at a corner. As they peer around the corner, they see Red Leaf flirting with the two clinic technicians. Red Leaf directs the men's attention away as the three quickly walk to the elevator and press the button. The doors open, they enter, and the doors close.

On the main floor, they walk past the front desk. They look over the desk to see two technicians still on the floor bound and gagged. One attempts to speak, but he only makes a muffled sound.

"I am a damn mountain!" Juicy Fruit proclaimed to them. He then laughs.

All three men burst through the front door where a rusty truck awaits them. Walks as a Bear is behind the wheel. The vehicle doors open, and the men jump inside as they lift Pale Moon to the seat.

They ride to the other side of the building and wait. A moment later, they see Red Leaf and Leaping Frog run out of a door. They jump into the back of the truck. With tires screeching, the truck quickly takes off down the road and out of the complex.

Leaping Frog loudly bellows an Indian battle cry. Juicy Fruit and Red Leaf join in.

* * *

It has been several weeks, and Pale Moon sleeps almost constantly in his tipi.

Big Feather often sits by his side praying and chanting softly. Sometimes, he blows smoke over Pale Moon's body in an attempt to, as he calls it, "rid him of the evil spirits that inhabit his body."

On the seldom occasions that Pale Moon wakes, he continues to remain confused over all that has happened to him. He opens his eyes wide and looks at Big Feather.

"Father, who am I really?"

"You are my son."

He then falls back to sleep.

One day, Morning Blossom visits Pale Moon. When she enters his tipi, Big Feather and Little Mouth smile at her, and then they leave them in privacy.

She kneels by his sleeping body and gently strokes his hair while she hums an ancient love song. Although he doesn't wake, a smile does come to his face.

The winter months pass. Pale Moon is awake more often. Little Mouth serves him a bowl of her squirrel soup while Big Feather sits beside him smoking his pipe.

As Pale Moon sips, his eyes fixate on the fire.

"My son, I know what is in your belly. Tell me what is in your mind."

"I was told that my real name is Brian Nance. I was being filled with venom by a man who said he was a doctor. The people in the fort thought they were doing me good. One man even told me that he was my brother. How can this be?"

Big Feather takes a long draw from his pipe. The smoke circles his head as he exhales.

"My son, there is no Brian Nance. Whoever that man is, he is gone now. All that remains is an Algonquin Indian named Pale Moon."

Epilogue

It is a hot July day, and the Indian village experiences the highest number of visitors ever. In fact, the entire beach park encounters a surge in beachgoers. As a direct result, the village generates a sizable income selling many of its manufactured goods. The village is so successful and in need of keeping accurate figures that Sleeping Elk is selected to serve as the village accountant. Prosperity is rich at the beach park and business booms for all.

At Amir's shop, Amir's daughters return from the village festivities dressed as Indians. The village has become so popular that a big seller at Amir's shop is tee-shirts that boast the printed image of tipis on a beach.

In the village, a new tipi sits near the center of everything. It features newly-painted images of leaping frogs and sleeping elk. Pale Moon emerges from this tipi, rested and regenerated. His face is close-shaven, his hair is trimmed, and his skin bares a deep, red tan. He wears a beaded deerskin robe, fringed leggings, moccasins, and a war bonnet of pale feathers. He has indeed undergone a physical transformation into an Algonquin Indian.

Pale Moon has also experienced a spiritual transformation as well. He feels psychologically fit and self-confident. Now, the young woman he has encountered in his dreams is forever gone. Whoever she was, he believes and hopes that she is now peacefully at rest.

The authorities were spotted by the Indians a few times canvassing the beach park and, every time they visited, the villagers would hide a barely recognizable Pale Moon and tell these men that the man they seek has moved out west to Lakota territory never to return. The men had no reason to believe them, but they also had no reason to doubt them. Every time they returned to their white van in the parking lot, they always found its tires slashed. They resorted to using a different vehicle—a gray sedan. However, they returned to this car only to find its tires slashed, too. This vandalism added to their frustration. Eventually, the men stopped coming.

Big Feather believes that his son will never be recaptured because the spirits protect him and render the white man blind to Pale Moon's presence.

Steve has also been visiting the beach park in hopes of seeing his brother. He often walks along the boardwalk, peering over the rails. But, he is always afraid to enter the village. He continuously fails to recognize his brother from his far-off perspective and especially because Pale Moon's transformation to an Indian has become so complete and so radical.

* * *

On one fine morning, right after the sun rises, Forest Water accompanies Morning Blossom to the ocean to bathe her in the surf so that she may receive the blessings of the earthly spirits. For, on this morning, she will marry Pale Moon.

The entire village is beautifully decorated for the special day. Excitement is abounding. A celebration of this kind has not occurred at the village since Walks as a Bear married Forest Water. The beachgoers themselves, saturating the boardwalk, show a special interest in the festivities.

At noon, the drummers signal the start of the ceremony.

Big Feather appears from his tipi. As chief, he is the one who will officiate over the marriage ritual. He is impressively dressed in traditional Indian clothing required for the occasion by tribal law. In one hand, he holds a spear adorned with several dangling beads and feathers, and in the other hand, he holds a customary ceremonial pipe.

The drum beats in slow cadence as the wedding sponsors—Walks as a Bear, Little Mouth, Forest Water, and Amir—present themselves before Big Feather. Big Feather raises his hands to the sky to call upon the good spirits. Then, he blesses the sponsors by speaking the words of the ancestors. He then addresses the villagers.

"My people, today is a good day! Today, we are joining two of our children together. It has been an ancient tradition to unit, prosper, and offer our thanks to the great creator. Let us now begin. I call upon my son."

Pale Moon emerges from his tipi. The villagers cheer as he walks by them. He presents himself before Big Feather and bows.

"Pale Moon, my son, is it your intention to marry?"

"Yes, father," he said with a trembling voice.

Big Feather notices that Pale Moon is very nervous.

"Relax," Big Feather said softly.

Morning Blossom emerges from her parents' tipi with Pink Rose. She wears a traditional wedding dress made by Falcon Eyes. She is also wearing a neckless Forest Water made that bears the shell that Pale Moon found on the beach on their first evening together. She approaches Big Feather and bows.

"Morning Blossom, is it your intention to marry?" Big Feather asked.

"Yes, father," she said.

"As the pipe bearer, I require you, my children, to pledge your love and commitment for one another before the great creator. There is no breaking this commitment, not even in death."

Big Feather lifts the pipe and offers it to Pale Moon. A burning twig is introduced to its bowl, and Pale Moon inhales the smoke. Big Feather then offers it to Morning Blossom who also inhales the smoke. Big Feather blesses them both. He then calls upon the sponsors.

"Do you declare your commitment to guide and help our children, Pale Moon and Morning Blossom, in their journey through life?"

"We do," they answered together.

Big Feather offers the pipe to them, he wields the burning twig, and they inhale the smoke. Big Feather then turns his attention back to Pale Moon.

"My son, you will now present your gift to your bride."

Pale Moon takes out the compass ring that he found long ago and presents it to Morning Blossom. He carefully places it on her finger.

"My people, I declare before you that our children, Pale Moon and Morning Blossom, are now husband and wife!"

The villagers erupt in cheers and cries. The visiting audience on the boardwalk applauds.

During the reception, tribal music fills the air. The drumbeating and chanting can be heard for miles. The villagers dance and feast on venison, squash, beans, corn, potato, and berries.

Leaping Frog, surrounded by the Pale Moon, Morning Blossom, Four Winds, Juicy Fruit and others, excitedly tells the story of the escape from the psychiatric center.

"When I was in the bed, I wrapped the sheets around my head so I can look out. A woman in white walked in, and I jumped up on the bed!"

The circle gushed in laughter.

"I did! She screamed so loud; pills went everywhere!" So, I ran out of the room and grabbed Red Leaf and we ran down the stairs and out the door!"

They continue to laugh.

Four Winds leans over to Pale Moon.

"Brother, will you walk with me?" he asked.

"Yes, brother."

Both men walk a short distance away.

"Pale Moon, I just want to say that I am proud to be your brother. I want to say that I am happy that Morning Blossom is part of our family."

"I am glad, brother."

"Me and Red Leaf are in love. We will marry. I hope that you will be a sponsor."

Pale Moon fills with emotion.

"I would be honored."

"I also want to say, Pale Moon, that I love you."

"I love you, too, Four Winds."

The men embrace.

"I heard that you fish better than Sleeping Elk," Four Winds said.

"Oh, yeah."

"Everyone fishes better than Sleeping Elk."

Both men laugh.

* * *

After the celebrations, Pale Moon and Morning Blossom walk out of the village to an awaiting horse. They mount the steed and look back. Little Mouth bellows a loud, yelping cry. All join in with cheers and cries. All wave at them.

The newly-married couple ride off passed flower patches and beyond the high hill where a lone tipi awaits them. They smile and consider it an appropriate honeymoon suite.

* * *

Steve, undetected, witnessed the entire wedding ceremony not realizing at first that his brother is the groom. He looks carefully at the Indian he knows to be Brian.

With all that he sees, he is struck with a sudden realization. He recognizes the fact that his brother may never be happier than where he is now. He knows that his brother is better off here rather than committed indefinitely in a psychiatric institution. He also understands now that he may never see his brother again. He is overwhelmed with emotion and calls out.

"Good bye, Brian! Good bye, Pale Moon!"

* * *

Several months later, Pale Moon and Morning Blossom sit on the sand by the village watching the tide drift away. They contemplate the many happy years that lie ahead, and they consider all of their dreams becoming reality. What adds to their excitement and anticipation is the child she bears that moves restlessly inside of her.

Life is there.